Home at Last

Read all of
MARGUERITE HENRY'S Misty Inn
books!

#1 Welcome Home!
#2 Buttercup Mystery
#3 Runaway Pony
#4 Finding Luck
#5 A Forever Friend
#6 Pony Swim
#7 Teacher's Pet
#8 Home at Last

Marguerite Henry's Misty Inn

Home at Last

By Judy Katschke

Illustrated by Serena Geddes

ALADDIN

New York London Toronto Sydney New Delhi

This book is a work of fiction. Any references to historical events, real people, or real places are used fictitiously. Other names, characters, places, and events are products of the author's imagination, and any resemblance to actual events or places or persons, living or dead, is entirely coincidental.

ALADDIN
An imprint of Simon & Schuster Children's Publishing Division
1230 Avenue of the Americas, New York, New York 10020
First Aladdin hardcover edition February 2018

Also available in an Aladdin paperback edition.

Book designed by Laura Lyn DiSiena
The text of this book was set in Century Expanded.
Manufactured in the United States of America 0118 FFG
10 9 8 7 6 5 4 3 2 1
This book has been cataloged with the Library of Congress.
ISBN 978-1-4814-6995-1 (hc)
ISBN 978-1-4814-6994-4 (pbk)
ISBN 978-1-4814-6996-8 (eBook)

For my Forever Friends

Home at Last

Chapter 1

"SPIDERS? BEETLES?" BEN DUNLAP ASKED. "What about bedbugs?"

Willa Dunlap looked up from her after-school snack to stare at her younger brother. "Do you have to talk about bugs," she asked, "while I'm eating peanut butter and crackers?"

"Okay, maybe not bugs," Ben went on. "But field mice could be a possibility."

"Mom," Willa told her mother as she walked into the kitchen, "make Ben stop."

"What's this about bugs, Ben?" Mom asked as she placed her laptop on the kitchen counter.

"You and Dad were talking about how there are no reservations for Thanksgiving weekend," Ben explained, "and it's only two weeks away. I was just trying to figure out why."

Willa's dad was busy preparing dinner for the two guests at the inn that week. It was November and the slow season at Misty Inn and the Family Farm Restaurant. But that didn't stop Chef Eric Dunlap from cooking up a storm.

"There are no creepy crawlies inside our bed-and-breakfast, Ben," Dad insisted. "Outside, but not inside."

"No mice, either," Willa said with a grin. "New Cat makes sure of that."

She picked up their pet cat and held him close. "Why don't we have guests for Thanksgiving weekend?" she asked. "We were totally booked solid in the summer."

"Everybody was here for the pony swim," Mom said.

Dad looked over his shoulder with a wink. "You did hear about the annual pony swim, Willa?" he asked. "When a herd of wild ponies swim across the bay from Assateague Island to Chincoteague?"

Willa knew her dad was teasing. The pony swim was world famous and the biggest event on Chincoteague Island. For the past ninety-two years.

"The pony swim is the best," Willa admitted. "But don't people want to see the wild snow geese that fly here in November? They're awesome too."

Dad's paring knife made thumping sounds on his cutting board as he diced celery. "Sure they are," he said. "But most people like to spend Thanksgiving with good friends and family, like the song says."

"What song, Dad?" Ben asked.

Dad stopped chopping. He cleared his throat, then belted out in a booming voice: "'Over the river and through the woods to Grandmother's house we go.'"

"Got it, Dad." Willa chuckled. "Except Grandma Edna and Grandpa Reed won't be over any rivers or through any woods this Thanksgiving."

She picked up a travel brochure Grandma Edna had dropped off the other day. "They'll be thousands of miles away in Hawaii."

"I can't picture Grandma and Grandpa in Hawaii," Ben said, shaking his head. "No way."

"Why not?" Mom asked.

"I don't think they even have bathing suits," Ben explained. "I've only seen Grandma Edna and Grandpa Reed in overalls and work clothes."

"Don't forget stethoscopes," Willa added. She was proud of her grandmother, who worked as a veterinarian on Chincoteague Island. She taught Willa everything she knew about horses and all kinds of animals. So much that Willa wanted to be a vet when she grew up.

"Well, it's about time my hardworking parents took a break," Mom said. "And maybe it's time we did too."

"What do you mean, Mom?" Willa asked.

"Since we have no reservations at the bed-and-breakfast over Thanksgiving weekend," Mom said with a smile, "your dad and I were thinking about taking a little family trip somewhere."

"*You* were thinking, Amelia," Dad pointed out. "I'd rather stick around Misty Inn in case guests drop by at the last minute."

All Willa heard was the word "trip." "A trip?" she asked excitedly. "You mean like Hawaii?"

"Bring on the surfing lessons," Ben said, sputtering cracker crumbs.

"Sorry, Ben," Mom said, shaking her head. "But the only thing you'll be surfing over Thanksgiving is the Web."

"Why?" Ben asked.

"The Hawaiian Islands are super far and we only have five days," Mom explained. "By the time we get there, it'll be time to fly home."

"Washington, DC, is doable," Dad suggested. "So is Philadelphia, and New York."

"I'd like to see the White House and the Smithsonian Institution," Willa said. "Let's go to DC, please."

"I vote for New York," Ben said, his hand shooting up. "I want to see the crazy-tall buildings."

"We used to live in Chicago, Ben," Willa

reminded him. "We saw crazy-tall buildings every day."

"Then I want to see the Thanksgiving Day Parade," Ben stated. "That's in New York every year, isn't it?"

Willa's eyes lit up at the mention of the famous parade. Ever since she was four years old, she had watched it on TV. But watching the giant balloons, marching bands, and floats from the sidewalks in New York would be even better.

"New York sounds good," Willa said.

Ben raced toward the door. "Start spreading the news," he said. "I'm going upstairs to pack for New York City."

"Whoa, Ben," Dad called.

"It's not definite yet," Mom said, "so hold your horses."

Whoa? Hold your horses?

The words made Willa blink hard. She wanted to take a family vacation, but there was someone much more important than New York or the parade. And she was waiting for Willa in the barn right now.

"Mom, Dad? What about Starbuck?" Willa asked about her pony. "Who's going to care for her while we're away?"

"I'm sure we can find someone responsible," Mom said. "Someone who can feed New Cat and Amos, too."

Willa knew feeding a cat and a puppy was hard work. But taking care of a horse was practically a science, like Grandma Edna always said.

"But I ride Starbuck every day," Willa said.

"I feed and groom her regularly too. She might get upset if I'm not here."

"So we're not going to New York City or the parade because of Starbuck?" Ben complained. "Seriously?"

Willa shot her brother a sharp glance. When Starbuck had showed up at Miller Farm with an injured leg, they had both helped Grandma Edna take care of her. But after Starbuck found her own way to Misty Inn, it was Willa who took charge—waking up early every morning to feed and groom Starbuck and coming home straight from school to ride her.

"Starbuck is my pony, Ben," Willa said. "You don't have a pony of your own, so what do you know about horses?"

"Wasn't that a bit harsh, Willa?" Dad asked.

Willa felt her cheeks burn. The last thing she wanted to do was hurt Ben's feelings. But taking back her words was like putting toothpaste back in the tube—almost impossible.

She was about to apologize when Mom piped in: "Kids, we don't know for sure if we're going anywhere, so let's all take a breather."

"Good idea," Dad agreed. "And until we know for sure, I'm going to cook Thanksgiving dinner as always."

"Eric, you're what?" Mom asked with surprise.

"We have to be prepared, Amelia," Dad said. "Any minute the phone can ring with Thanksgiving reservations—"

BRRRRRRRIIIIIIINNNG.

All four Dunlaps froze at the sound of the kitchen phone.

"Too weird," Ben said.

"Totally," Willa agreed.

Mom walked over to the ringing phone. "It's Miller Farm," she said, looking at the caller ID. "Your grandfather can't stop talking about visiting Pearl Harbor soon."

Answering the phone, Mom put it on speaker. It wasn't Grandpa Reed, but Grandma Edna.

"Amelia, you're not going to believe what's happening," Grandma Edna said. "Never in a million years."

"Dad wants to sign you guys up for hula lessons," Mom guessed.

"As if that's going to happen." Grandma Edna chuckled. "The last dance I learned was the twist."

Ben wrinkled his nose. "The what?"

"Tell us what happened, Grandma Edna," Willa called toward the phone. "Is it something to do with one of the animals?"

"No, honey," Grandma Edna replied. "I just got a call from a friend who lives up the island."

Grandma Edna paused a few seconds, then

said, "There's a wild pony in her apple orchard plucking apples right off her prizewinning apple tree."

"A pony?" Willa said with surprise. Any news about a pony was huge. Especially when it was a wild pony like Starbuck.

Chapter 2

"WHERE DID THE PONY COME FROM?" WILLA asked, leaning toward the phone, still on speaker. "Is it short and shaggy like a Chincoteague pony?"

"I just know it's male and loves apples so far," Grandma Edna replied. "But I do need your help."

"Our help?" Ben said excitedly. "This is getting good."

"The pony, until we find his owner, will need a safe place to say," Grandma Edna went on. "There's no empty stall at Miller Farm at the moment. And I don't want to introduce a wild horse to the pasture herd until we get to know him better."

"So you want us to keep the pony in our pasture?" Willa asked. "Maybe he can have the stall right next to Starbuck's."

"Willa, slow down," Dad said. "Other than that he likes apples, we don't know very much about this pony yet, like Grandma Edna said."

"Can we meet him?" Willa asked her parents.

Mom gave it a thought. She then shrugged and said, "I suppose."

"Dad?" Willa asked hopefully.

When her father nodded yes, Willa said,

"Awesome. Will you be there too, Grandma Edna?"

"I'm afraid not, honey," Grandma Edna said. "One of the horses here at the farm is upchucking from eating too many weeds. I don't want to leave him just yet."

There was a slight pause before Grandma Edna added, "Which is another reason I want you to take in this horse."

"Is he throwing up too?" Ben asked, wrinkling his nose. "Gross."

"No, but he might get sick if he eats too many apples," Grandma Edna explained. "Apples can be hard on a horse's digestive system, especially a Chincoteague pony's."

"Why a Chincoteague pony?" Willa asked.

"For hundreds of years, horses were mainly

grass eaters," Grandma Edna explained. "Their digestive systems evolved to process small grass meals over the course of a day."

"That's why horses like to graze," Ben said. He shot Willa a smirk. "See? I do know something about horses."

Willa smirked back. Was it just more than a year ago that her little brother was too shy to speak?

"Since the Chincoteague ponies have been isolated on Assateague Island for hundreds of years," Grandma Edna went on, "they aren't accustomed to different foods like apples."

"I'm glad I'm not a Chincoteague pony," Ben said, grabbing a shiny red apple from a bowl. "I love a good Winesap apple."

"Okay, everybody," Grandma Edna said. "If

you're going to rescue that renegade pony, you'd better do it before it gets dark."

"Good idea," Mom agreed. "That pony may not want to follow us home in the dark."

"Unless he follows Starbuck," Willa blurted. "Let me ride Starbuck to the apple tree. The pony might feel more comfortable around other horses."

"Or more jittery," Mom said.

"It's worth a try, Amelia," Grandma Edna said. "Worse comes to worse, Willa can just turn Starbuck around."

"Thanks, Grandma Edna!" Willa exclaimed.

Grandma Edna ended the call. Mom turned to everyone and said, "Looks like Operation Pony Rescue is all systems go."

The Dunlaps sprang into action. Mom hung

up a BE BACK SOON sign in case new guests showed up while they were gone. Dad washed a few baby carrots to feed the wild pony—instead of apples.

"Here's the address," Mom said, showing Willa a map she had printed out. Willa studied the map and nodded. She knew exactly where Grandma Edna's friend lived.

"Oh, and take the phone, too," Mom said, handing the family's extra phone to Willa. "Call me immediately if you can't find the house."

"I'll be there," Willa said. "First I have to saddle Starbuck."

Willa stopped at the kitchen door, remembering Ben. "Do you want to come with me to the barn?" she asked.

"Me?" Ben scoffed. "I don't have my own

pony, so what do I know about horses?"

Willa heaved a sigh as she stepped out the door. *Sarcastic much?*

Amos the puppy rushed over to Willa, then scampered after her to the barn. The moment the doors were open a crack, Amos flitted inside.

Closing both doors, Willa heard Starbuck shake her mane and nicker. She turned and walked over to her stall with a smile.

"Hey, girl," Willa said, petting her pony's butterscotch-colored forehead with the pretty white star mark. "I know I came by after school, but we have an important job to do."

Starbuck blew air out of her nostrils. The pony's warm breath on her arm comforted Willa as it always did. She looked over at the empty stall next to Starbuck. The last pony to stay there was the Starlings' pony Buttercup.

Sarah Starling was Willa's best friend. In a very short time Starbuck and Buttercup became good friends too.

"You might get a new barn mate, Starbuck," Willa explained, swinging open the stall door. "I don't know much about him, except that he loves apples."

After loosely tying Starbuck to the hitching post, Willa gave her pony's back a quick but thorough groom. She then pulled on the saddle pad, followed by the much heavier saddle. Making sure to fasten the saddle to Starbuck's girth, Willa gave it a safety and comfort check.

"You're good to go, girl," Willa said, unhitching her pony. "Now, let's meet your roomie."

The Dunlaps' car had already left by the time Willa rode Starbuck toward the road. Other cars slowed down as they passed Willa and Starbuck ambling along the sandy roadside.

Glancing down, Willa could see more leaves on the ground than on the trees. It was the second week in November and growing dark early like Grandma Edna said. Were the runaway pony's owners wondering where he was? Were they worried about him?

"I hope you never get lost, Starbuck," Willa said as they sauntered up the road at a gentle pace. “But if you do, I hope someone helps to bring you straight home.”

Willa had no problem finding the house where Grandma Edna’s friend lived. The woman’s name was Farrah. She had long gray hair worn in a single braid down her back. And by the time Willa joined the others, she was frantic.

"I did approach the pony several times," Farrah was in the middle of telling Mom and Dad, "but he kept turning his rump to me."

Willa dismounted Starbuck, holding her harness. Ben stood next to his sister, filling her in on what she had missed: "The tall, skinny guy next to Farrah is her neighbor. His name is Jerry."

"The pony turned his back on me, too," Jerry was saying, his eyes wide. "Was it something I said?"

"No, no." Mom chuckled. "That's just a horse's way of saying he's not interested in you."

"Nothing personal," Dad added.

Farrah's house stood in the middle of a small but well-planted apple orchard. The branches were almost bare but dotted with bright, shiny, late-fall apples.

"Where's the pony?" Willa whispered.

"There," Ben said.

Willa looked to see where Ben was pointing. Tucked away in the orchard was an apple tree with low-hanging fruit. Standing beneath it, nibbling away on an apple, was a chestnut pinto gelding with a shaggy light-brown mane. The stocky little pony had four white patches circling his ankles. They made it look like he was wearing socks.

That's got to be a Chincoteague pony, Willa thought excitedly. *Just like Starbuck.*

"How do you think I feel," Farrah was wailing, "watching my prizewinning apples turn to horse chow."

"Prizewinning, huh?" Dad joked. "At least we know the pony has good taste."

But Farrah didn't laugh. Didn't even smile.

"Just stop that apple-eating renegade," Farrah said. "Please?"

"Let me try," Mom said.

Willa and Ben watched quietly as their mother approached the pony. Like Willa, Mom knew never to approach a horse from behind, which might startle him and make him kick. Instead, she spoke gently as she approached, keeping a good distance to his side.

"Hey, boy," Mom cooed, "is that apple good?"

But before Mom could get near—

"There he goes again," Jerry said. "He's turning his back on her, too."

Quickly Mom stepped back to avoid a possible kick.

"You see?" Farrah wailed, her apple-shaped

earrings swinging as she shook her head. "It's hopeless. Soon all my apples will be gone."

Still holding on to Starbuck, Willa turned to her parents. "Let me walk Starbuck over to the pony," she said. "Maybe he'll respond to her."

"Go ahead," Mom said. "Just give yourself and Starbuck enough distance."

Willa gripped Starbuck's reins as she led her toward the apple tree. "Look, boy," she called gently to the horse. "Someone wants to say hi."

But the other horse did not. With his rump to Willa, he took another step back. So did Willa and Starbuck.

"Maybe we should call Grandma Edna." Willa sighed.

"But Grandma Edna's with a sick horse," Mom said.

"I know, Mom," Willa said. "But if we don't get that pony away from the apples, there'll be another sick horse."

Mom nodded as she pulled out her phone. "I'll call her now." While she stepped to the side to make the call, Dad forced a smile in the direction of Farrah.

"So," Dad said cheerily, "what kind of apples do you grow here?"

"The pony is eating from an old-fashioned Winesap tree," Farrah explained blankly. "They ripen later than most apples, which is why they're still on the trees."

"Winesap are my favorites," Ben piped in.

"They bake well in a pie too," Dad said.

Farrah nodded. "They're very hearty," she said, "and can survive the first cold snap."

"But not a hungry horse," Jerry muttered.

"Jerry, please," Farrah scolded.

Dad seemed relieved when Mom walked over with a big smile.

"Good news," Mom said. "When I told my mother about the pony, she said she'd be here lickety-split."

"'Lickety-split' is Grandma Edna talk for 'real quick,'" Willa said. "Right, Ben?"

But when Willa looked out from behind Starbuck, Ben was no longer beside her. Instead, he was walking straight toward the pony.

"Ben, what are you doing?" Willa called. She turned frantically to her parents and said, "Get him back before the pony kicks—"

"Wait." Dad told Willa. "The pony isn't turning his back to Ben."

"What?" Willa said. She whirled around to see Ben standing alongside the pony stroking his neck. The pony shook his shaggy mane, then turned to nudge Ben's shoulder.

"Will you look at that," Farrah said. "I wonder why he has no problem with the boy."

"Maybe because he's shorter," Mom speculated. "And doesn't show any fear."

"I didn't show any fear," Willa said as she watched Ben stroke the pony's neck. "And I'm not much taller than Ben either."

"At least the pony stopped eating the apples," Dad pointed out. "That's the most important thing."

Apples. Willa smiled as she remembered the apple Ben had eaten at the house.

"Maybe," Willa said, "the pony is relaxed because he smells apple on Ben's breath."

"Or maybe," someone with a familiar voice said, "it's because the pony likes him."

Chapter 3

EVERYONE TURNED TO SEE GRANDMA EDNA walking over from her pickup truck.

"That was quick," Mom told her own mother.

"Why so surprised?" Grandma Edna asked. "When I say lickety-split, I mean lickety-split."

Grandma Edna smiled at Ben, who was petting the pony's shaggy mane. "Well, now," she said, "isn't Ben the junior horse whisperer."

"I guess," Willa said softly.

It was hard for her not to be a little jealous of her brother. She was supposed to be the horse expert, not him.

But Dad is right, Willa thought as she watched the pony nuzzle Ben's shoulders. *At least he stopped eating the apples.*

"The pony's coloring . . . and the four white socks," Grandma Edna said. She narrowed her eyes as she studied the pony. "I feel like I've seen that horse before, but I can't pinpoint where or when."

Grandma Edna shook the thought out of her head and said, "Willa? Did you bring a halter and a lead rope?"

"Got them," Willa said, happy to be useful.

She reached into Starbuck's saddlebag and pulled out the nylon halter and lead rope.

"Thanks," Grandma Edna said, taking both accessories. "Now let's get Johnny Appleseed away from that tree."

Willa smiled at Grandma's made-up name for the horse. But what was his real name?

Ben stepped to the side as Grandma Edna approached with the halter. The pony became a bit skittish as Grandma Edna slipped the halter over his head. After attaching the lead rope, Grandma Edna gave it a tug. The pony grunted, not moving an inch.

"Here we go again," Farrah groaned.

"Let me try, Grandma Edna," Willa said. She turned to her mother. "Mom, hold Starbuck while I—"

"Look," Jerry said. "The boy is leading the horse."

"What?" Willa gasped. She turned toward Ben and her eyes widened. Her brother truly was leading the stubborn little pony away from the apple tree.

"You really have a way with horses," Farrah told Ben as he led the pony toward them. "I'll bet you want to be a veterinarian just like your grandma when you grow up."

"How did you guess?" Ben said with a big smile.

Willa frowned. Since when did Ben want to be a veterinarian? *She* wanted to be a veterinarian. Ben still wanted to be a ninja warrior—or a waterslide tester.

"Now, how are we going to get Johnny Appleseed to Misty Inn?" Mom asked.

"I suppose the only way is to have Ben lead him," Grandma Edna replied.

"Yes," Ben said under his breath. He turned to ruffle the front of the pony's mane. "Hear that, Winesap? We're a team."

"'Winesap'?" Dad repeated.

"After the apples he was eating," Ben explained. "And my favorite apples too."

"But Grandma Edna called him Johnny Appleseed," Willa told Ben. "Isn't that a cute name for a pony?"

"Cute?" Ben scoffed. He looked the pony straight in the eye and said, "Nod once for Winesap, twice for Johnny Appleseed."

Everyone laughed as the pony bobbed his head once.

"Okay—I saw you tug his halter," Willa complained.

"Did not," Ben said.

"Did too," Willa said back.

"Kids, kids," Grandma Edna said. "I think Farrah would like some closure to this afternoon. So what do you say you get Winesap to Misty Inn?"

"Good idea," Mom said. "I'm just not sure I want Ben walking along the road with a strange pony."

Ben opened his mouth to protest when Willa said, "Ben can follow me and Starbuck, Mom. Johnny Apple—I mean, Winesap—seems to be comfortable with us."

"Sounds like a plan," Mom said. "You have the phone, right?"

"Yup," Willa said, patting her jacket pocket.

"Mom? Dad?" Ben asked, holding Winesap's lead rope. "What's going to happen to Winesap when we go on vacation?"

Grandma Edna appeared surprised. "Vacation?" she asked. "What's this about a vacation?"

"We were thinking of going away for a few days," Dad answered, "while the kids are off for Thanksgiving."

"Well, phooey kablooey," Grandma Edna said. "I was going to ask you guys to feed and check in on the animals while Reed and I are in Hawaii."

"But I thought you were hiring a young vet tech for the animals at Miller Farm," Mom said. "His name is Jason?"

"It's Jaden, and he just got engaged." Grandma Edna sighed. "He's going down to North Carolina for Thanksgiving to meet the parents."

"That's so sweet," Mom said with a smile.

"Sweet for him, not for me and Reed," Grandma Edna muttered. "Who am I going to get to care for the animals on the farm now?"

"Maybe we don't have to go away," Ben blurted.

Willa stared at Ben as if he had three heads. "What about the Thanksgiving Day Parade in New York?" she asked.

"We can watch it on TV," Ben said with a flap of his free hand. "Who wants to stand out in the cold for three hours and have to use a porta potty?"

Ben turned to give the pony a pat. "Besides . . . I'd rather spend Thanksgiving with this guy."

Winesap tossed his head and whinnied.

"Actually," Mom said, "I was having second thoughts about traveling over Thanksgiving. Buying tickets so close to the holiday will be very expensive."

"And you know I have trepidation," Dad

agreed. “What if we get last-minute reservations?”

Mom put her hand on Grandma Edna’s shoulder. “Don’t worry, Ma,” she said. “We’ll take good care of your animals while you and Dad are in Hawaii.”

“And I will take good care of Winesap,” Ben said, giving the little pony a hug. “Right, boy?”

As Winesap snorted, Willa took a deep breath. “Can we go home now . . . please?”

Grandma Edna gave Winesap a quick checkup. “He may get diarrhea from all those apples,” she said. “Call me if it lasts more than eight hours.”

“Diarrhea? Seriously?” Ben asked.

“Do you still want to take care of him?” Willa teased.

On the way to her pickup truck, Grandma Edna looked over her shoulder and said, "I'm going to make some calls back at the farm. To see what I can find out about that pony."

After saying good-bye to Farrah and Jerry, the Dunlaps and the horses were on their way. Mom and Dad drove slowly up the road. Willa and Ben walked along the sandy curb together with Starbuck and Winesap.

"I don't get it, Ben," Willa called back. "When I wanted to stay home with Starbuck, you acted like I was from another planet."

"That was before I got Winesap," Ben answered.

"Got Winesap"? Willa furrowed her brow as she and Starbuck led the way. *Does Ben think Winesap is his pony?*

Willa was about to explain to Ben that Winesap probably had another owner. But when she looked back and saw the big grin on her brother's face, she changed her mind.

"I don't want to leave Starbuck over Thanksgiving either," Willa said. "And taking care of the animals on Miller Farm will be fun."

Ben didn't answer. He was too busy whispering sweet nothings into Winesap's ear. Willa decided to do the same thing—with Starbuck.

"Winesap does seem like a good horse," Willa told her pony softly, "but I still like the name Johnny Appleseed better."

By the time the Dunlaps returned to Misty Inn, the November sky was a deep, dusky purple. Dad went from the car straight to the kitchen.

Mom greeted Willa and Ben as they walked the ponies up the driveway.

"We should take the ponies to the barn," Willa suggested. "I want to show Winesap his new stall."

"Not the stall yet for Winesap, Willa," Mom said. "We don't know if he'll take to a strange barn."

"But I told Starbuck she'd have a new roomie," Willa said. "And the weather's getting colder."

"And I don't want Winesap to catch a cold," Ben said. He wrinkled his nose and added, "On top of his diarrhea."

"His stomach is fine for now, Ben," Mom said. "And nature gave him a nice thick coat to protect him from the cold."

Mom pointed to the distance and said, "Let's

put Winesap in the paddock. That's what Grandma Edna does at Miller Farm with unidentified horses."

"But he is identified, Mom," Ben insisted. "He's Winesap."

Mom walked alongside Winesap as Ben led him to the field. Willa walked Starbuck to the barn. She could tell her pony was tired from such a busy day. So was Willa.

After feeding and watering Starbuck, Willa groomed her pony's coat until it shone.

"Everyone knows you swam here from Assateague Island, girl," Willa said as she closed the stall door. "But where did Winesap come from?"

Starbuck blinked a soft brown eye.

"I don't know either." Willa sighed. "But

until we find out, looks like you've got the place all to yourself."

Willa left a tuckered-out Starbuck and the barn. As she passed the field, she glanced at Winesap. His shaggy brown tail was swinging calmly as he watched her walk by.

Looks happy to me, Willa thought.

Willa expected to see Ben at the fence. Instead, she found him in the kitchen. His eyes were wide as he listened to Mom speaking on her phone.

"Really?" Mom was saying. "That's too bad."

"What's going on?" Willa asked Dad.

"It's Grandma Edna," Dad said as he warmed up a seafood casserole for the inn's two guests. "She made some inquiry calls about the pony. I'm guessing she had no luck."

Mom shook her head as she ended the call.

"No pony with Winesap's description is missing from the Virginia Assateague herd," she said.

"Oh!" Ben exclaimed. "Too bad."

Willa could see Ben frowning—but his eyes were dancing with delight.

"Grandma Edna is waiting to hear from the Pony Rescue," Mom went on. "She says we shouldn't get our hopes up too high."

"Okay," Dad said, slipping on an oven mitt. "So what do we do next?"

"We give Winesap some space," Mom said firmly, "until we know his history."

Willa understood what that meant: They shouldn't interact with Winesap.

From the grin on Ben's face, Willa had a feeling he understood too—in a whole different way.

Chapter 4

"COVER YOUR MOUTH WHEN YOU YAWN, BEN," Willa said. "I don't want to see Crunchy Munchy cereal crumbs all over your tongue—it's gross."

Ben snapped his mouth shut. It was Monday morning as he and Willa waited for the school bus.

"I had a granola bar for breakfast, smartie," Ben insisted. "And I'm tired because I woke up super early to check in on Winesap."

Willa knew that was true. On her way to the barn that morning, she had seen Ben in the pasture feeding and watering Winesap. At one point the little chestnut pony nudged Ben's arm with his shaggy head.

Seeing Ben with Winesap made Willa happy and a bit sad at the same time: happy that Ben was bonding with a pony, sad at the thought of her little brother becoming a horse expert too. Would Ben soon know more about horses than she did?

Ben's voice interrupted Willa's thoughts. "It's awesome to get my own pony," he said, "and it's not even my birthday."

"You know, Ben," Willa said, pretending to look down the road for the school bus. "While you were still out with Winesap, I was talking to Mom."

"So?" Ben asked, gazing back at the field and Winesap.

"So Grandma Edna spoke to someone from the Maryland herd over the weekend," Willa explained. "She's still waiting to hear if anyone there recognizes the picture of Winesap she e-mailed them."

Ben shrugged. "Grandma Edna already spoke to the Virginia herd," he said. "And they didn't recognize him."

"Right, but there are two herds of wild ponies on Assateague Island," Willa explained. "They're separated by a fence at the Virginia and Maryland line."

Ben started rolling his eyes as Willa said, "The Virginia herd is owned by the Chincoteague Volunteer Fire Company, and the Maryland herd is owned by the National Park Service."

"Duh—as if I don't already know," Ben said. "What are you all of a sudden? Willa-pedia?"

"Very funny." Willa sighed.

"Besides," Ben said with a smile, "from the looks of him, Winesap probably is a wild pony with no owners."

"Nuh-uh," Willa said. "Winesap is a gelding."

"So?" Ben asked.

Willa smiled. She was the horse expert after all.

"A gelding is a horse who has had surgery," Willa explained. "Wild ponies usually don't have surgery."

"What kind of surgery?" Ben asked.

"Um," Willa said, "maybe Grandma Edna better explain that."

To change the subject, Willa reached into the side pocket of her backpack. She pulled out a tight roll of papers and said, "Look what I made up last night to help Winesap."

"Help him how?" Ben asked.

Willa waved a proud hand over the flyer she'd designed and printed. Above Winesap's picture were the words, "Do You Know Me?" Underneath was a description of Winesap along with Misty Inn's phone number and e-mail address.

"I don't see Winesap's name on it," Ben said.

"That's the name you gave him," Willa told him. "For all we know his real name is Charlie or Champ or Chestnut."

"Whatever." Ben sighed. "It's not like Winesap is going to stick anyway."

"What do you mean?" Willa asked, stuffing the papers into the backpack.

"You're the one who keeps saying I'm not going to keep him," Ben mumbled.

Willa was glad when the school bus rolled down the road. Convincing Ben that Winesap had another home was like convincing a crab to buy sand.

Ben trailed Willa onto the bus. Halfway up the aisle they separated to sit with their best friends, Sarah and Chipper Starling.

"Guess what?" Willa asked, slipping into the seat next to Sarah. "We're going to be in town this Thanksgiving with no guests at Misty Inn. Zero, zip, zilch."

"So?" Sarah asked.

"So maybe I can finally have a sleepover at Misty Inn," Willa said excitedly. "With all the empty rooms, I can invite every girl from our class—"

"Sounds awesome, Willa," Sarah interrupted. "But I won't be able to go."

"Why not?" Willa asked. "Don't tell me you're going to Hawaii too?"

"I wish." Sarah chuckled. "It's my cousin Paisley. She's visiting from California this Thanksgiving, and she's our age."

"Paisley can come to my sleepover too,"

Willa said excitedly. "Then she can hang out with us the rest of the weekend."

"Can't." Sarah shook her head. "We haven't seen Paisley since we were eight years old, so my parents want us to do stuff as a family. The whole weekend."

Willa's heart sank at the news. "Oh," she said. Sarah flashed a smile, eager to change the subject. "What's happening with that wild pony you e-mailed me about last night?" she asked. "His name is Fuji, right?"

"Wrong apple. It's Winesap," Willa said, smiling. "And I made up these flyers to help find his owners."

Willa lifted her backpack from the bus floor. But when she looked inside the side pocket . . .

"That's weird," Willa said, sticking her hand

deep inside. "I rolled them up and slipped them in here. Now they're gone."

"Maybe they fell out before you got on the bus," Sarah said. Her eyes suddenly lit up. "Hey, if the wind blows them all over town, you won't have to hand them out."

Unless the flyers didn't fall out, Willa told herself. *Unless someone doesn't want to find Winesap's real owners.*

Turning in her seat, Willa caught Ben staring guiltily straight at her. *And I think I know who that someone is.*

Chapter 5

"DAD, WHERE'S BEN?" WILLA ASKED AS SHE pulled a grilled cheddar cheese sandwich from the microwave oven.

It was Friday afternoon. Willa had just finished her math and science homework and needed a pick-me-up before writing a book report.

Willa liked to finish Friday's homework before the weekend. This way she could concentrate on Starbuck instead of decimals, fractions, and the solar system.

"Um . . . Dad?" Willa asked again. "Did you see Ben?"

"Ben?" Dad asked. His back was to Willa while he stared at the laptop on the counter. From where Willa stood, she could see it was open to his favorite recipe site, Hip, Hip, Gourmet! "I think he's outside with Winesap."

Surprise, surprise, Willa thought, taking a bite of her sandwich. Ben had hardly said two words to Willa since her flyers went missing from her backpack—probably because two nights ago Willa had found them in the recycling bin behind the house.

Willa was so mad, she wanted to scream—but she didn't. She knew Ben didn't want

Winesap's real owners to be found.

"Sarah told me her family is having company over Thanksgiving," Willa had told Ben as they walked up from the bus today, "so Sarah and Chipper will be too busy to do stuff with us."

Willa expected Ben to share her disappointment. Instead, he shrugged, smiled, and said, "That's okay. I'll spend Thanksgiving with my new best friend—Winesap."

Glancing out the window, Willa saw Ben feeding Winesap blades of grass through the fence.

Ben thinks he knows a lot about horses, Willa told herself, *but I know something he doesn't know.*

Dusting toast crumbs from her hands, she thought, *I know what's best for ponies. And finding Winesap's real owners is best for him.*

"Willa?" Dad asked, interrupting her thoughts. "I can't decide on a side dish for Thanksgiving dinner. Do you prefer squash casserole with pineapples and walnuts or broccoli au gratin?"

"Does 'au gratin' mean melted cheese?" Willa asked.

"You mean like the grilled cheese sandwich you just ate?" Dad teased. "Sort of."

"Then I vote for broccoli," Willa declared.

Dad tapped his fingers on the counter. "Your mom likes the squash recipe," he said. "So I'll make both. Along with the string-bean dish everybody loves."

Squash casserole, broccoli, *and* string beans?

"Um . . . Dad?" Willa asked slowly. "No guests are checking in to Misty Inn for Thanksgiving . . . so why all the food?"

"You never know who might drop by," Dad said with a grin. "Better safe than sorry, right?"

"Sure," Willa said, smiling too. They might not have guests for Thanksgiving, but they would have an awesome dinner. And broccoli with melted cheese.

As Willa rinsed her plate in the sink, she noticed a sheet of paper on the counter. At the top of the page in Dad's elegant handwriting was the word THANKSGIVING. Along the sides were doodles of cornucopias.

Willa tilted her head to look closer. It was a Thanksgiving menu with turkey, two kinds of salads, mashed potatoes, sweet potatoes, shoestring fries—even tofu turkey with quinoa stuffing. At the bottom of the list were five desserts, including two kinds of pie—pumpkin and apple.

"Two pies, Dad?" Willa asked.

"Maybe one will do," Dad said. "The other can be a chocolate or coconut cream cake."

"If it's one, please make it pumpkin," Willa said. "Pumpkin is my favorite even when it's not Thanksgiving."

"Just so you know," Dad said, "your brother voted for apple."

"As in Winesap?" Willa sighed.

Gazing out the window, she watched as Ben petted Winesap through the fence. It made her want to spend time with her own pony doing what they loved best. . . .

"See you later, Dad," Willa said with a little wave. "I'm riding Starbuck to the beach."

It was gray and cold by the time Willa and Starbuck reached the island's sandy shore. The dramatic weather made the snow geese and crashing waves seem even more awesome to Willa.

She looked across the bay to Assateague Island, tall grass swaying in the wind. The island and its wild ponies made her think of Winesap.

"I don't get it, Starbuck," Willa told her pony. "Don't Winesap's owners want him back?"

The thought made Willa sad. She waited until Starbuck finished nibbling a clump of sea grass, then gently steered her around. Starbuck seemed to know the way home, walking up the beach to the trail that led straight to Misty Inn.

Ben was still standing in the field as Willa rode Starbuck up the driveway. He was too busy with Winesap to notice Willa dismounting and leading Starbuck to the barn.

"That's weird," Willa said aloud as they

neared the barn. "I know I closed the doors before we left, so why are they open?"

Stepping inside the barn, Willa saw why. Her mom was inside the barn rummaging through the shelves.

"Hi, Willa," Mom said, still rummaging. "I was just seeing what tools we have in here."

"Why, Mom?" Willa asked as she removed Starbuck's saddle. "Is something broken?"

"No," Mom said, dropping a box of nails into a canvas bag. "If we're not having guests for almost a whole week, I thought I'd work on some fixer-upper projects."

"But I thought you were going to relax over Thanksgiving," Willa said. "You know, put your feet up and binge-watch your favorite TV shows."

"There's plenty of time to be lazy," Mom

said, "after I hang up new towel racks in the guest rooms."

Willa walked Starbuck into her stall. As she filled a water pail, Mom said, "Willa, I'm worried about your dad and Thanksgiving."

"Dad has been acting so happy lately," Willa pointed out, "like a pig in mud, Grandma Edna always says."

"He may be acting happy," Mom said, "but he's got to be upset about no guests over Thanksgiving."

"Why, Mom?" Willa asked.

"Your dad is a chef," Mom explained. "Back in Chicago he loved cooking Thanksgiving dinners at the hotels he worked in."

"I remember," Willa said with a smile. Dad used to bring home the most awesome leftovers at night. It was like having two Thanksgiving dinners in one day.

"Cooking a small family dinner can't be enough for him," Mom said. "He'll probably cook a ton of food, and we'll have more leftovers than ever."

Willa shrugged and said, "Then you'll have one more project, Mom."

"What's that?" Mom asked.

"Finding charities to give the extra food to," Willa said with a smile.

"Why didn't I think of that?" Mom asked. She was about to give Willa a hug when they both heard a loud squeal.

"It sounds like Ben," Mom said. "I'll go outside and see what's up."

Willa placed the full water bucket in Starbuck's stall. "Ben better not be scaring

Winesap, Starbuck," she said. "That's the last thing a lost pony needs."

After closing the stall door, Willa left the barn. She caught up with her mom, who suddenly stopped short. Willa followed her gaze to the field. That's when she froze too. Her brother was lying flat on the ground—Winesap standing over him.

"Oh no," Willa cried. "Ben!"

Chapter 6

WILLA'S MIND RACED AS SHE TOOK A STEP toward the field. What if Ben was badly hurt? How could she forgive herself for being a downer about Winesap? But then Mom grabbed her arm and said, "Wait."

"But, Mom," Willa began to say, "Ben is—"

"Just listen," Mom said softly.

To what? Willa turned her face back to the

field. She strained her ears, and heard a sound that wasn't a squeal at all. It was the sound of Ben giggling.

Willa took another step and looked closer. Ben was now on his knees, still giggling as Winesap seemed to lick his face. He reached into his pocket and held out his hand, flat like

Grandma Edna had taught them. Winesap lowered his head, nibbling what looked like string beans.

"Hey." Ben giggled again. "That tickles."

Willa smiled. She was glad her brother was okay and that Winesap was being gentle. But when Willa looked up at Mom, her brows were furrowed with worry.

"What's the matter, Mom?" Willa asked. "Ben is having fun with Winesap."

"Too much fun," Mom admitted. "What's going to happen when we find Winesap's real owners?"

"I know," Willa said with a nod.

"Remember when we moved to Chincoteague?" Mom asked. "Ben was shy and quiet as a mouse."

"How can I forget?" Willa asked with a grin. "Ben could stand behind me for minutes without me even knowing."

"But then Ben and Chipper became friends," Mom pointed out. "And now Ben can hardly stop talking." Mom watched Ben lovingly stroke Winesap's muzzle. "What if finding Winesap's owners sends Ben back into his shell?"

Willa could tell she was worried. She didn't want that to happen either. "Maybe Ben shouldn't spend so much time with Winesap," she suggested. "I can tell him I need help with Starbuck."

"Don't interrupt their fun," Mom said with a sigh. "Not until we have to."

Willa knew what that meant, and she watched her mom walk back to the house.

Even Mom knows getting Winesap back to his real home is the right thing to do, Willa thought as the sound of her brother's laughter rang in her ears.

It was then that Willa knew how she would spend the weekend. After finishing the book report that was due on Monday, she would return to her other assignment: looking for Winesap's real owners.

"Your cherry cobbler was awesome, Dad," Willa said at dinner that night. "And speaking of dessert, I think I'm in the mood for apple pie this Thanksgiving."

"Awesome," Ben exclaimed. "Maybe we can have ice cream on top too."

Dad looked up from his place at the table.

The last guests had left that afternoon, so the Dunlaps were having a private dinner in the Family Farm dining room.

"Willa, just before you were campaigning for pumpkin pie like it was running for president," Dad said. "Why the sudden switch to apple?"

With a smile at Ben, Willa said, "I guess all that talk about apples made me crave some."

Deep inside, Willa knew the real reason. Choosing Ben's favorite pie for Thanksgiving made her feel just a bit less guilty about finding Winesap's real owners.

"After we eat pie, we can watch the *Boa Boy* marathon on TV," Willa suggested. "It's on every Thanksgiving."

Ben's eyes popped wide open at the mention of his favorite TV superhero. "Seriously, Willa?"

he asked. "You once said you'd rather get a cavity drilled than watch *Boa Boy*."

Mom was surprised too. "Apple pie, *Boa Boy*," she said. "Are you feeling okay, Willa? There is a bad cold going around."

"I feel good, Mom," Willa said cheerily. *Guilty . . . but good.*

"Well," Dad said, leaning back in his chair, "I for one am looking forward to a nice small Thanksgiving dinner right here with my family."

Mom and Willa traded looks. Dad sounded convincing. But so was his mile-long Thanksgiving menu in the kitchen.

Willa was finishing the last of her cherry cobbler crumbs when the kitchen phone rang. "I'll get it," she said, standing up with her plate.

"If it's a guest, let me know," Dad said, his eyes flashing. "Right away, Willa, okay?"

Hurrying into the kitchen, Willa glanced at the caller ID. It wasn't a guest, but her other best friend, Lena. She placed her dish in the sink with one hand and picked up the receiver with the other.

"Hi, Lena," Willa said. "What's up?"

“You tell me,” Lena said.

“Huh?” Willa asked.

“That wild horse your family found,” Lena said. “Did you find his owners yet?”

Willa forgot that she’d told Lena about Winesap at school that week. “No,” she said. “I’m going to help Grandma Edna look for them this weekend.”

“And I am going to help *you*,” Lena declared.

“Help me? How?” Willa asked.

“A missing horse is a mystery,” Lena explained. “And who is better than solving mysteries than me?”

Chapter 7

"I DON'T WANT BEN TO KNOW WHAT WE'RE doing, Lena," Willa said. "If he finds out we're trying to find Winesap's owners, he'll just get upset."

"So this mission is top secret," Lena said, her dark eyes flashing. "Even better."

Both girls huddled before the desktop computer in Misty Inn's office. It was Saturday,

but Lena was over bright and early to solve "the mystery of the mysterious pony," as she called it.

"Did you hand out flyers?" Lena asked.

"Long story, but no," Willa replied.

"Flyers are boring, anyway," Lena said. "Did you try a pet psychic?"

"A . . . what?" Willa asked.

"Pet psychic," Lena explained. "There's a woman in Indiana who can tell you what your pet is thinking without even meeting him."

Willa smiled. Lena was great at solving mysteries although sometimes her methods could be a bit far out.

"No pet psychic," Willa said, "Let's try some old-school ways first—"

"Hey, the door's locked," Ben interrupted as he rapped on the locked door. "What are you guys doing in there?"

Willa and Lena traded panicky looks.

"No big deal, Ben," Lena called toward the door. "We're just watching . . . um . . . dumb, cartoony videos."

"No, Lena," Willa hissed. "Ben loves cartoony videos—even the dumb kind."

Too late. Ben was tugging at the doorknob, trying to get in. "What kind of cartoons?" he demanded.

"Um," Lena said. "Er—"

"*Sparkle Ponies*," Willa lied.

After a moment of silence Ben said, "No, thanks. . . . I don't feel so good anyway."

Willa and Lena listened to the sound of Ben's footsteps trailing off.

"That was close." Willa sighed with relief.

"Let's get to work," Lena said, facing the computer. "What do you know about Winesap so far?"

"He's short, stocky, and shaggy like the ponies from Assateague Island," Willa explained, "so he probably came over with the pony swim."

"When?" Lena asked.

"Good question," Willa said. "Grandma Edna was here early this morning to look at Winesap's teeth."

"His teeth?" Lena asked, scrunching her nose in confusion. "What do his teeth have to do with anything?"

"A horse's teeth can tell a vet how old he is," Willa explained. "Grandma Edna told us that Winesap is probably between eight and twelve years old."

"That's a huge difference," Lena said. "When I was eight, I couldn't do a lot of things I can do now. Like ride a skateboard, swim backstroke, eat with chopsticks—"

"Lena," Willa said, "we're talking about a horse, not a human kid."

"Right," Lena said. She pointed to the computer. "There's a special website for lost pets in Chincoteague. Let's see if anyone reported a missing pony."

Willa nodded and said, "I forgot to tell you that Winesap has four white socks. Not real socks, the color of his coat."

"Got it." Lena smirked as if to say "duh."

Willa opened the lost-pet site. The home page had pictures of lost pets of the week and their information. There was a German shepherd named Lancelot, a cat named Caramel, a bunny named Trixie—even a pet rat who went by the name of Whiskers. But no missing pony.

"What makes a pony run away from home anyway?" Lena wondered out loud.

"If a gate is left open, a pony can run out

of fear, like if he hears loud thunder," Willa explained. "They also run away out of curiosity or when they're bored."

"When they're bored," Lena repeated excitedly. "Let's search for the most boring places on Chincoteague and ask if they're missing a pony."

"Let's not." Willa giggled. "Instead, let's search to see if any missing ponies have been reported this morning."

Willa and Lena made several searches for missing ponies on Chincoteague or the nearby mainland. After searching for fifteen minutes, they found no new clues.

"Now what?" Willa groaned.

Lena drummed the chair arm with her fingers thoughtfully. "There's a site where you upload your picture," she said, "then see which famous celebrity you look like."

"What does that have to do with a missing pony?" Willa asked.

"Easy," Lena said. "We upload Winesap's picture to see if he looks like a missing celebrity horse."

Willa stared at her friend. Did Willa just hear what she thought she heard?

"I think I have a better idea, Lena," Willa said. She smiled as she turned back to the computer. "Let's watch *Sparkle Ponies*."

"Cool," Lena agreed.

Willa and Lena spent the next half hour watching videos and voting for the most adorable kittens on a site called Cutie Kitties. After Lena left for her Saturday gymnastics class, Willa joined Dad in the kitchen.

"Wow," Willa said under her breath upon seeing Dad's menu for Thanksgiving dinner. It had grown to two whole pages.

"Question," Dad said as he stood over a much-used cookbook on the counter. "For Thanksgiving, should I add anchovies to the Caesar salad?"

Willa scrunched her nose. "You mean those hairy little fish?"

"I'll take that as a no." Dad chuckled.

Willa pointed to Dad's menu. "Are we really having three salads on Thanksgiving?" she asked. "For just the four of us?"

"As I said, you never know who might drop by," Dad replied. He glanced back at the book and said, "Croutons. Garlic or the regular kind?"

"You choose, Dad," Willa said as she gazed out the window.

Winesap seemed to love being out in the paddock. Early that morning Willa had brought Starbuck to the field to join him. The ponies seemed happy to see each other again—rounding their necks and putting their heads together.

"Where's Ben?" Willa asked. "I'm surprised he's not outside with Winesap."

Dad took on a serious tone. "I'm not surprised," he said. "Ben came down with a fever. He's in the living room with your mom."

"A fever?" Willa asked. No wonder Ben had said he wasn't feeling well.

Willa found Ben in the living room wrapped in a blanket on the recliner chair. Mom looked concerned as she studied a thermometer.

"Under a hundred and one." Mom sighed. "Looks like you caught that cold that's going around, Ben."

"I'll bet you caught a cold out in the field," Willa told Ben, "by sitting on the chilly ground yesterday while you were playing with Winesap."

"I wasn't just sitting," Ben said, his voice

hoarse. "I walked Winesap around the field too."

Ben pulled a tissue from a box and said, "When we got tired, I'd read to Winesap—standing up."

Willa blinked with surprise. "You read to Winesap?" she asked.

Ben blew his nose with a honk, then said, "He likes science fiction."

Mom turned to Willa. "You can't catch a cold from a damp, chilly ground," she explained. "It takes exposure to germs."

Ben shot Willa a look that said, *You see?*

"I'll get a cool compress for your forehead, Ben," Mom said. She paused at the door. "Oh, before I forget, Grandma Edna called again this morning."

Ben's eyes grew huge with worry. "Did she find Winesap's real owners?" he asked.

Willa held her breath, waiting for Mom's answer.

"No real owners yet," Mom said. "Grandma Edna said you should start getting Winesap's stall ready. They're predicting snow next week."

"That means Winesap's going to stay," Ben exclaimed as best he could with a fever. "I may feel like poo, but this is my lucky day."

Willa raised an eyebrow at Ben. Why was he getting excited about Winesap moving into the barn? It wasn't like he was moving into the inn. Or into Ben's room.

But as Willa left for the barn to get the stall ready, she knew the real reason. With each day, no real owner meant Winesap might stay for good.

I like Winesap too, but it's just not right, Willa thought. *A pony needs to be with his or her real owners, so we have to find them.*

She walked to the field and leaned against the fence. Starbuck's ears pointed in her direction as her tail swished at flies. Willa couldn't see Winesap's ears—that's how shaggy his mane was.

"Okay, Mr. Socks," Willa said with a smile as Winesap padded toward the fence. "If you're moving in next to my pony soon you need to look respectable."

Winesap reached his shaggy head over the fence and nuzzled Willa's shoulder.

"That means you need to be groomed," Willa told the pony gently. "When was the last time your owners did that?"

With a new goal, Willa raced to the barn. In

a flash she was back in the field with a bucket full of grooming brushes: a currycomb, stiff and soft brushes, and one for Winesap's mane and tail.

Starbuck nickered as Willa opened the fence and walked inside. But this time she wasn't there for her own pony. She was there for Misty Inn's unexpected guest.

After placing the bucket on the ground, Willa pulled out the currycomb. Standing on Winesap's left side, she moved the brush in a circular motion to loosen the dirt.

"There you go, boy," Willa said gently. "It's getting cold, but soon you'll be in a nice, warm, cozy stall."

While she was brushing, Willa's eyes darted around the field then to the house. Standing at the window of his room was Ben. Her brother's hands rested on the windowpane as he watched her and Winesap.

Willa sighed to herself as she turned back to her brushing. The longer it took to find Winesap's owners, the harder it would be for Ben.

"Who are you really, Winesap?" Willa asked softly. "I wish you could tell me."

Chapter 8

"NOW I'M GOING TO GET HAT HAIR," SARAH complained as she tugged at the plushy white hat on her head. "I hate that about winter."

Willa turned to Sarah, who was sitting next to her on the school bus. It was Monday and the first really cold day of the year. Practically all the kids on the bus were bundled up in hats, scarves, and woolly gloves. Sarah had on a hat designed to look like a black-and-white panda head.

"Who cares about hair when you can wear neat hats like yours?" Willa asked with a smile. "And I like winter, especially when it snows."

"And when I get to wear my cool snow boots!" Sarah said, smiling too.

Willa rubbed a clear spot on the frosty bus window and looked outside "It's not snowing yet," she said, "but there might be an early snowstorm right before Thanksgiving."

"I heard," Sarah said. "My parents said the airport might shut down, and you know what that means."

Willa sure did. It meant Sarah's cousin Paisley couldn't fly in from California.

"Weather reports can be wrong sometimes,"

Willa blurted. She felt horrible for feeling a tiny bit glad. Without Paisley, Sarah would be free to spend Thanksgiving weekend with her.

"Where's Ben?" Sarah asked. "He didn't get on the bus with you this morning."

"He's home with a cold," Willa explained. "But I'm sure he's planning a great escape so he can visit Winesap."

"Winesap," Sarah said, rapping her forehead. "I can't believe I forgot to tell you."

"Tell me what?" Willa asked.

"I showed my dad the picture you e-mailed me of Winesap," Sarah explained. "He said he thought he recognized the horse from one of the pony swims."

"No way." Willa gasped at the news.

Mr. Starling was what Chincoteague Islanders

called a saltwater cowboy. They were the skilled cowboys who led the herd of Assateague ponies across the bay to Chincoteague every July.

"My dad said Winesap might have swum over from Assateague nine years ago," Sarah said.

"Wow," Willa said. "How did he remember Winesap?"

Sarah shrugged. "Something about the marks around Winesap's ankles," she said, "the ones that look like white socks."

Willa felt her heart thumping excitedly inside her chest. "Was Winesap sold at the pony auction?" Willa asked.

Each summer the pony swim was followed by an auction, where Assateague ponies were sold to the highest bidders.

"Dad didn't say," Sarah admitted. "But

Winesap must have been sold or else he would have been herded back to Assateague."

Willa drew in her breath as she leaned back in the seat. The pieces of the pony puzzle seemed to be falling into place, although they still didn't know who the pony's real owners were.

"Sarah, your parents let you take a phone to school, right?" Willa asked.

Sarah nodded and said, "For emergencies. Why?"

"I think I have an emergency," Willa said. "May I borrow it to call my grandmother, please?"

"I guess," Sarah said. She pulled out a small flip-phone and gave it Willa. "Just don't let the other kids see it or everyone will want to borrow it."

"Deal," Willa said. Ducking down in her seat, she keyed in Grandma Edna's number. She waited until—

"Miller Farm," Grandma Edna chirped.

"Grandma Edna, guess what?" Willa whispered. "Winesap swam here from Assateague Island nine years ago. Sarah's dad told her so."

"Nine years ago?" Grandma Edna said. "It's a great start, honey. I'll check my old vet records and make some calls."

"You're the best, Grandma Edna," Willa whispered. She ended the call and handed the phone to Sarah. "Thanks for the phone—and the scoop."

"Aren't your grandparents going to Hawaii for Thanksgiving?" Sarah asked. "How are they going to go if they shut down the airport?"

"I hope they still go," Willa said with a

smile. "*After* Grandma Edna finds Winesap's real owners."

That day at school the kids were super excited about Thanksgiving vacation in just three days. Willa was excited about that and about something else. She couldn't wait to see what Grandma Edna would find out about Winesap.

After school Willa raced home from the bus, careful not to slip on freshly formed ice. She swung the door open and smiled. Sitting at the kitchen table with a cup of coffee and a plate of cookies was Grandma Edna.

"Now, here's the girl I was waiting for," Grandma Edna said before taking a sip of coffee.

"What happened, Grandma Edna?" Willa

asked as she pulled off her winter woollies and draped them over a chair.

"Hello to you too," Grandma Edna joked. She put down her mug and said, "You'll be happy to know that Sarah's tip paid off."

"Paid off? How?" Willa asked. "Did you find Winesap's owners?"

"Sure did," Grandma Edna said. "Winesap is owned by a woman named Marjorie Lundgren. Her house is about a half a mile from Farrah's house."

"Where we found Winesap." Willa gasped.

"The Lundgrens used another vet here on Chincoteague," Grandma Edna said. "But I was called one night about nine years ago when he was out of town. That's why Winesap and his description were in my files."

Grandma Edna bit into a cookie, then said, "I didn't think to go back so far in my files. Good thing I did."

Willa was glad Grandma Edna finally found Winesap's owners, but there was still something she didn't get. . . .

"Why didn't Marjorie look for Winesap?" Willa asked. "Didn't she know he was missing?"

"Not until Marjorie got back to Chincoteague last night," Grandma Edna explained. "She was in Richmond on an extended business trip. The teenage girl checking in on Winesap was too embarrassed to report him missing."

"Wow," Willa said under her breath.

"The pony belongs to Marjorie's son, Matt, who's away at college," Grandma Edna went on. "She admitted to me that Matt outgrew the pony."

"How can anyone outgrow a pony?" Willa asked.

"Matt became busy with college and his part-time jobs," Grandma Edna explained, "but he was too attached to the pony to sell him."

Willa took a cookie from the plate. "What's Winesap's real name?" she asked.

"I don't know, Willa," Grandma Edna said. "I never wrote the pony's name in my file, just his description. And Marjorie only called him the pony."

Mom walked into the kitchen, holding a bottle of green cough syrup. Willa guessed it had been for Ben.

"How is Ben, Mom?" Willa wanted to know.

"Feeling better but not quite one hundred percent," Mom replied. She looked at her own mother and asked, "So when is Marjorie picking up the pony?"

"Her son is coming home for Thanksgiving break," Grandma Edna explained. "She said they'd come to Misty Inn after the weekend to claim the pony."

Willa's eyes widened at the news. The mystery pony was a mystery no more. So why wasn't Willa happy about it?

"Mom?" Willa asked slowly. "Who's going to tell Ben? About Winesap's owners, I mean."

"Your dad is out food shopping before the snow," Mom said with a frown. "So I guess I'm stuck with the task."

"Oh, I'll do it," Grandma Edna said, standing up. "I've had animals come and go on Miller Farm for decades."

As she headed toward the door, Grandma Edna added, "It's not like I have to be home packing. With that big ol' storm brewing, our trip to Hawaii isn't looking very good."

Willa picked up the plate of cookies, then followed Grandma Edna and Mom up the stairs. Ben was reading in bed when they filed into his room. His nose was bright red from rubbing it with tissues.

Ben looked up from his book. When he saw Willa, Mom, and Grandma Edna standing at the foot of his bed, he frowned.

"Uh-oh," Ben said with a croaky voice. "Is this about Winesap?"

Chapter 9

GRANDMA EDNA SAT DOWN ON THE BED NEXT to Ben. "I did just get some news," she said gently. "And it is about Winesap."

Willa watched as Grandma Edna told Ben all about Marjorie Lundgren and her son. As Ben listened, his nose grew redder and he began to sniff. His eyes watered up too.

Was it his cold? Or the news about Winesap?

After Grandma Edna finished talking, Mom said, "You know it's okay to cry about Winesap, Ben."

Ben gave a loud sniff then forced a little smile. "It's cool, Mom," he said. "If Winesap has other owners, he should go home to them."

Willa stared at Ben. Was it really okay? And would Ben blame her for trying so hard to find Winesap's real owners? She sure hoped not.

"Grandma Edna?" Ben asked. "What's Winesap's real name?"

"We don't know yet," Grandma Edna replied.

"Good," Ben said with a little nod. "So until they pick him up, he's still Winesap."

Mom leaned over to feel Ben's forehead. "You're much cooler now. How do you feel?"

Not answering, Ben's eyes zeroed in on the

plate in Willa's hands. "Are those chocolate chip cookies?" he asked with a sniff.

"With macadamia nuts," Willa said.

"Then I feel much better," Ben declared.

When Willa saw Ben's smile, she felt better too.

"Chocolate chip cookies with macadamia nuts," she said, "coming up."

"There you are, Willa," Ben called as he hurried up the driveway Tuesday afternoon. "I thought you'd never get here."

Willa blinked snowflakes from her eyelashes as she walked up toward the house. Was she seeing what she thought she was seeing? After he'd stayed home from school for another day, what was Ben doing out in the cold?

"The bus drove slowly in the snow," Willa said. "Do Mom and Dad know you're outside?"

Ben was so bundled up, he could hardly nod his head. His voice was muffled from the thick scarf wrapped around his neck and mouth as he said, "It's okay as long as we work fast."

"Doing what?" Willa asked.

"Getting Winesap into the barn before the snow gets heavier," Ben said. "Mom said I could do it as long as you help."

Willa could see light snow coating Winesap's horse blanket. She had borrowed the blanket from Starbuck that morning to keep Winesap warm.

"Let's do this," Willa said. She slipped both arms through the straps of her backpack to free her hands. Then she and Ben walked against the wind toward the field and Winesap. The chestnut pony blew wind from his nostrils as they filed through the gate.

"His halter is still on," Willa pointed out. "One of us has to get a lead rope."

Ben rolled his eyes as he pulled a coiled-up rope from his jacket pocket. "What does this look like?" he asked.

Willa smiled at Ben's preparedness. She still considered herself the pony expert, but Ben was catching up pretty fast.

The snow began falling more heavily as Ben attached the rope to Winesap's halter.

"You lead him," Willa told her brother. "I'll open the gate."

Winesap fell into step next to Ben as he led him through the gate. Willa ran ahead to open the barn doors.

"Company's coming, Starbuck," Willa called as she entered.

Speaking softly, Ben guided Winesap into the barn. The two ponies nickered at each other like old friends.

"Home sweet home, Winesap," Willa said.

"At least through Thanksgiving weekend." Ben sighed.

After removing the blanket, Ben led Winesap

into the empty stall near Starbuck. Ben stood inside the stall at Winesap's side as he turned him around to face the door.

"Good job, Pony Whisperer," Willa teased good-naturedly as Ben left the stall, closing and latching the door behind him.

Ben smiled as Winesap and Starbuck traded friendly snorts over the wall.

"I've got five whole days with Winesap before his owners pick him up," Ben reported. "If the snow doesn't get too high, maybe I'll saddle him for a ride."

"Maybe," Willa said. Together she and Ben hung up the heavy horse blanket. They were about to fill the water buckets when Mom stepped inside.

"I was about to go back to the house, Mom," Ben said. "I feel good. Really."

"That's not why I'm here, Ben," Mom said. "I came with good news and bad news."

"Good news first," Willa said.

"Schools are closed tomorrow because of the coming snowstorm," Mom said with a smile. "You guys have an extra day off for Thanksgiving break."

When Willa and Ben didn't react, Mom cocked her head. "So . . . aren't you happy about that?" she asked.

"Sort of," Ben said. "After being cooped up in the house since the weekend, I wanted to go back to school. I haven't seen Chipper in ages."

"Our new lunch lady Mrs. Wainwright promised us a

Thanksgiving dinner for lunch tomorrow," Willa explained. "There'd be hot, open-faced turkey sandwiches with cranberry sauce and sweet potatoes."

"Well, I thought that was the good news." Mom chuckled.

"What's the bad news, Mom?" Ben asked.

Mom's smile turned into a frown. She took a deep breath then said, "The Lundgrens aren't coming for Winesap after Thanksgiving weekend."

Ben's eyes lit up as he said, "They're not?"

"No, Ben," Mom said carefully. "They're coming tomorrow morning."

Chapter 10

THE BIG LACY SNOWFLAKES FROM THAT MORNING were now a blur as they began falling faster and heavier.

"Dad is inside cooking up a storm," Willa said.

"Do you have to say 'storm'?" Ben asked. "If it wasn't for this dumb snowstorm, I'd have a whole long weekend with Winesap."

"Sorry," Willa said.

It was Wednesday morning. Willa and Ben stood on the porch waiting for the Lundgrens to arrive. But Ben was in no hurry. . . .

"Maybe the Lundgrens' car will get stuck in the snow," Ben said, "for the whole weekend."

"Ben, that's horrible," Willa said.

But she couldn't blame her brother for being sad. Just yesterday he was over the moon to have Winesap all weekend. Today he was getting ready to give him back.

Mom had done her best to explain why: "Mrs. Lundgren is afraid the storm will keep her from picking up Winesap on Sunday. So she wants to drive Winesap home in the trailer tomorrow after her son gets home from college."

Ben had stared at Mom, then said in a soft voice, "I'm not feeling so well again."

With that, Ben left the barn, hurried straight to the house and up to his room. Later Willa had knocked on his door with a dinner tray, but Ben pretended to be asleep.

This morning Ben seemed better but still not over it.

"Grandma Edna and Grandpa Reed probably hate this storm too," Willa told Ben. "Their flight to Hawaii was canceled."

The sudden sound of crunching gravel and ice made Willa and Ben turn toward the driveway. Through a haze of snowflakes, Willa and Ben watched a Jeep drive up the shoveled driveway. Hitched to it was a small horse trailer.

"Great," Ben muttered under his breath.

Mom walked outside, zipping her down jacket. As Mrs. Lundgren got out of the car with Matt, Mom said, “Here they are. Let’s get it over with.”

Mom carefully stepped down from the porch. She walked ahead to the Lundgrens, Willa and Ben trudging behind.

“Well, hello, Dunlaps,” Mrs. Lundgren greeted, squinting through the falling snow. “First off, thank you for taking such good care of Crispin.”

“Crispin?” Ben asked.

“Isn’t that the name of an apple?” Willa asked.

“Sure is,” Matt said. “After we got Crispin at the pony auction, he would lean over the fence to eat apples from our neighbor’s tree. I thought naming him after an apple would be a good fit.”

"I named him Winesap," Ben said. "I mean, for while he was here."

"Winesap?" Mrs. Lundgren repeated.

"Seriously?" Matt asked.

Willa held her breath. Would they make fun of the name Ben chose? Instead—

"What a unique name for a pony," Mrs. Lundgren said.

"Why didn't I think of that one?" Matt chuckled.

Mom rubbed her gloveless hands together and said, "The snow is really coming down. Would you like to see Winesap?"

"Lead the way," Mrs. Lundgren said cheerily.

Ben and Willa followed Mom and the Lundgrens to the barn. They passed the field now covered with snow. Willa knew she'd miss seeing Crispin there.

"Here we are," Mom said, pulling open the barn doors.

Willa could see Starbuck's ears tilt toward them as they filed inside. Crispin gave a hearty whinny, then tossed his mane.

"Looks like someone is happy to see you," Mom told the Lundgrens.

Matt walked straight to Crispin's stall. "Hey, boy," he said softly as he stroked the pony's muzzle. "Whatcha been doing while we were away?"

"Listening to stories," Ben blurted.

"Stories?" Matt asked.

"Winesap—I mean, Crispin—loves science fiction," Ben explained. "I read to him every day except when I got sick."

Ben walked to Crispin's stall. He ruffled the pony's mane and said, "He also liked the music

I played him on my dad's phone. Mostly classic rock."

"Crispin likes rock?" Matt asked with a grin. "No way."

"Ben took good care of Crispin," Willa told the Lundgrens. "Really good care."

"I can see that," Mrs. Lundgren said. "You know, Ben, you can visit Crispin any time you want."

"Thanks . . . but no, thanks." Ben sighed. "It would be too hard to keep saying good-bye."

Everyone stared silently at Ben. Until Matt said, "Mom, I think I found a new home for Crispin."

"Where, Matt?" Mrs. Lundgren asked.

"Here at the Dunlaps'," Matt said, smiling at Ben. "The little dude reminds me of me when I got Crispin."

Willa gave a little gasp. She turned to Ben, whose jaw had dropped a mile.

"You mean . . . you want to give me Crispin?" Ben asked.

"Sure," Matt said. "I still have two years of college left. Then I'll probably move to the city."

Matt smiled at Crispin and said, "Can't exactly keep a pony in a studio apartment, right?"

"Right," Willa said, smiling. Ben was too excited to say another word.

"Well, I think it's a super idea," Mrs. Lundgren said.

Ben turned to Mom. "Can I keep him, Mom?" he asked excitedly. "Please?"

"It's fine with me," Mom said. "And I'm pretty sure it'll be fine with your dad, too."

Ben pumped a joyous fist in the air.

"Woo-hoo!" he shouted. "I've got my own pony."

Willa smiled as she watched her brother, happy at last. His dream of owning Winesap had just come true, and it would be an amazing Thanksgiving. Now, if only her dad's dream of having a huge Thanksgiving dinner would come true too. . . .

"Mrs. Lundgren?" Willa asked slowly. "What are you and Matt doing for Thanksgiving?"

"Aloha, Grandpa Reed," Willa said, slipping a plastic purple lei around her grandfather's neck.

"Does this mean I have to play the ukulele?" Grandpa Reed joked.

"You never played the ukulele, so don't start now," Grandma Edna warned.

Willa giggled. It was her idea to have a

Thanksgiving luau, ever since her grandparents' flight to Hawaii was canceled. All the guests at the long Family Farm community table wore a lei—the Dunlaps, the Millers, the Lundgrens, and the Starlings.

"Paisley would have loved a Thanksgiving luau," Sarah said. "I can't believe her flight was canceled too."

"Well, it was nice of you to invite us to the Family Farm for Thanksgiving dinner," Mrs. Starling said.

"And me and Matt," Mrs. Lundgren piped in. She turned to Dad, who was placing bowls of hot biscuits on the table. "Eric, I sure hope you didn't cook all this for us."

"But I'm glad you did, Dad," Ben said.

"Yeah," Chipper said, rubbing his stomach.

"I'm so hungry, I can eat a horse."

Grandma Edna raised an eyebrow. "Excuse me?" she asked.

Chipper gulped, then quickly added, "I mean—I'm as hungry as a horse. Yeah, that's it."

"Just make sure you leave room for dessert, Chipper," Dad said. "We have apple pie and pumpkin."

"Perfect," Willa declared.

Everything *was* perfect as she admired the table decorated with tiki lanterns, pineapples, plastic palm fronds, and—of course—the Dunlaps traditional paper-turkey centerpiece named Harvey.

Everyone was laughing, eating, and sharing what they were thankful for. Willa was almost certain Ben was thankful for Crispin. And in time he would become a horse expert too.

But I still know what's best for Crispin, Willa thought as she reached for a biscuit. *And the best place for Crispin—is with Ben.*

ACKNOWLEDGMENTS

Thanks to the entire Aladdin team for bringing this book to life. Karen Nagel's enthusiasm and humor make any project a pleasure. Thanks to her and to Fiona Simpson for trusting this lifelong city girl to imagine life on Chincoteague Island. Much thanks to Kristin Earhart for her wonderful vision of Misty Inn and its characters. Her knowledge and love of horses were incredibly helpful and inspiring. Thanks also to Serena Geddes, whose illustrations bring so much sparkle to the series, and to Laura Lyn DiSiena, for beautifully designing the series. Last but not least, a huge thanks to my family and forever friends—you're always there to lend support and an occasional ear for my ideas, day or night.